Foods We Eat

CHAPTER 13

How Do We Get Food?

How do we get apples?

Roberto and Ana like apples.

Do you like apples?

Apples grow on trees.
People pick the apples.

Trucks bring the fruit to stores.

Why do trucks carry the apples?

Some food comes from farms.

Vegetables and fruit grow on farms.

People put the vegetables and fruit in crates and boxes.

Refrigerated trucks bring the vegetables and fruit to stores.

Workers unpack the vegetables and fruit.

Why are there so many vegetables and fruits?

5

Some food comes from factories.

wheat

corn

rice

oats

Wheat, corn, rice, and oats are grains.
Cereal is made from grains.

Cereal is made at a factory.

The cereal is packed in boxes.

Trucks bring the cereal to stores.

What kind of cereal do you like?

What Comes First?

What comes first?
What comes next?
What comes last?

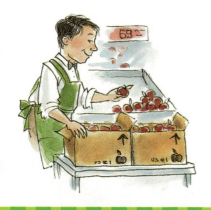  

Tell what you learned.

1. Where do apples grow? Touch the picture.

2. How do vegetables and fruit get to the supermarket?

   Say the name. Touch the picture.

3. Draw your favorite cereal.

CHAPTER 14

Let's Make a Meal!

How do we cook at home?

We chop the carrots.

We wash the lettuce.

We make a salad.

We cook together at home.

We set the table.

We eat together at home.

This family likes to eat together. How do you know?

Who cooks in a restaurant?

Many people cook in a restaurant.

One cook puts food on plates.

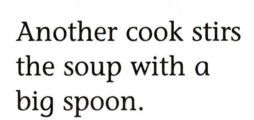

Another cook stirs the soup with a big spoon.

Everything is bigger at a restaurant.

The restaurant feeds many people.

12

Many people eat in a restaurant.
A waiter brings the food to the table.

What foods can you eat at a restaurant?

What foods can we make?
How can we make cheese sandwiches?

Start with a slice of bread.

Add cheese.

Add lettuce.

Put another slice of bread on top.

Cut the sandwich.

We made the sandwiches.

You can make a cheese sandwich, too.

Just follow the recipe!

What other kinds of sandwiches can you make?

Name them.

Tell what you learned.

1. Touch a kitchen tool.

2. Touch a food you eat in a restaurant. Say its name.

3. Draw a food you can make.

CHAPTER 15

Food Around the U.S.A.

Does everyone eat the same food?

David's family lives in New York.

They like turkey and potatoes.

Patty's family lives in Kansas.

They like meat and salad.

Manuel's family lives in San Francisco.
They like vegetables, fish, and rice.

What does your family like to eat?

What is your favorite food?

Alberto likes carrots.

He likes peas, too.

Sara's favorite vegetable is broccoli.

Kelly likes strawberries.

She likes peaches, too.

Bobby's favorite fruit is pineapple.

What vegetables do you like?

What fruits do you like?

Do you like corn?

tamales

corn on the cob

cornbread

corn chowder

popcorn

Corn is good in different foods.

Which corn food do you like?

Game Time

Choose a Meal!

Plan a meal.

Choose a main dish, a vegetable, and a fruit.

Name the foods.

Tell what you learned.

1. Who is eating corn? Show me.
2. The girl is eating her favorite fruit. What is it?
3. Draw your favorite food.